CHICO RODRIGUEZ

PAGE PUBLISHING, INC.
Conneaut Lake, PA

First originally published by Page Publishing 2020

ISBN 978-1-68456-317-3 (pbk)
ISBN 978-1-68456-318-0 (digital)

Printed in the United States of America

To do more, be more, give and laugh more. Never take anything for granted and imagine all the possibilities.

Dedicated to my girls Kiley, Avi, and Eliana, who inspire me each and every day.

Love, Dad

Hippidy-doo-rah-roo-ray! We get to go to the lake today.

We need our bait before it's late, oh how I can hardly wait!

We must dig before we jig. I hope we'll catch something big.

Squish! Squash! Scrunch! We dig and dig beneath the soil to find the squirmy wormy.

We grab our gear, and fish are near. It's so great to be out here.

A juicy jig beneath my bobber is what I wish the fish will clobber.

I see a duck. I see a boat, but I don't see my bobber afloat!

I think it took my worm and hook.
Now it's time to jerk the line!

Reel and reel, I finally feel the perfect cast at last. *Splish! Splash! Thrash!*

We'll let it go so it can grow, but soon I know we'll have to go.

One last cast is all I ask! Oh how I wish for one more fish. Oh how I wish for one more fish.

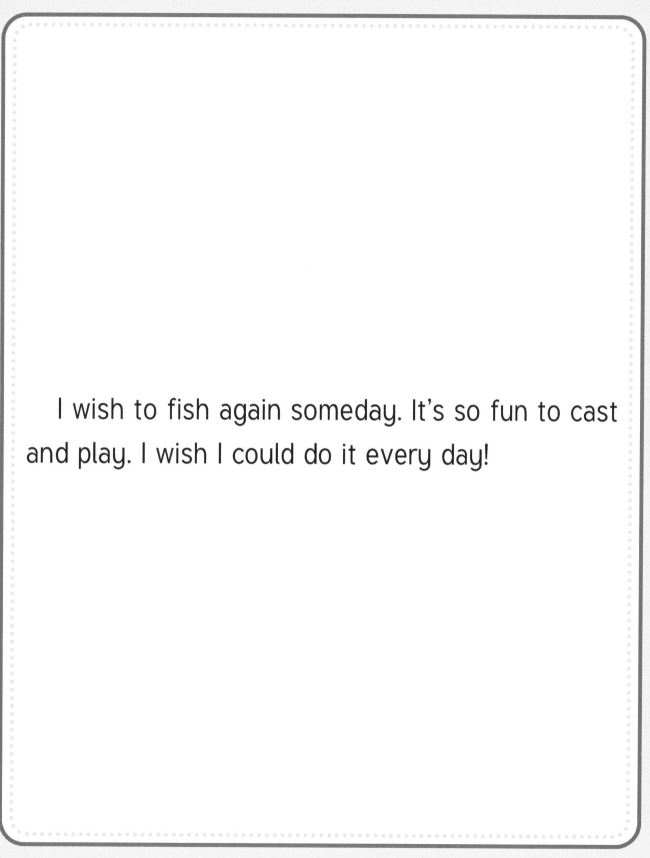

I wish to fish again someday. It's so fun to cast and play. I wish I could do it every day!

I love to see the waves crash.
I love to feel the fish thrash.

I love to hear nature call, but I think that most of all...

I'm just glad to be with Dad.

The End

FISH AND WHAT FISH LIKE

THE CLINCH KNOT

SIMPLE RIGGING

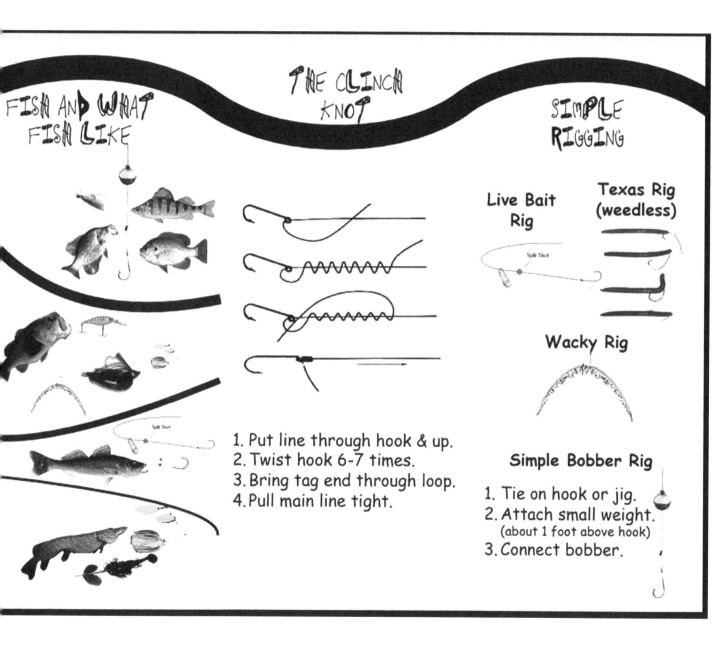

Live Bait Rig

Texas Rig (weedless)

Wacky Rig

1. Put line through hook & up.
2. Twist hook 6-7 times.
3. Bring tag end through loop.
4. Pull main line tight.

Simple Bobber Rig

1. Tie on hook or jig.
2. Attach small weight.
   (about 1 foot above hook)
3. Connect bobber.

CPSIA information can be obtained
at www.ICGtesting.com
Printed in the USA
BVHW022208270421
605960BV00003B/87

9 781684 563173